HERO

A WAR DOG'S TALE

BY JANE A.C. WEST
ILLUSTRATED BY SEB CAMAGAJEVAC

Titles in Full Flight 7

Badger Publishing Limited
Suite G08, Business & Technology Centre
Bessemer Drive, Stevenage, Hertfordshire SG1 2DX
Telephone: 01438 791037   Fax: 01438 791036
www.badgerpublishing.co.uk

Hero: A War Dog's Story ISBN 978-1-84926-267-5

Badger Publishing would like to thank Jonny Zucker
for his help in putting this series together.

Publisher: David Jamieson
Editor: Danny Pearson
Design: Fiona Grant
Illustration: Seb Camagajevac
Printed and bound in China through Colorcraft Ltd., Hong Kong

HERO

A WAR DOG'S TALE

CONTENTS

Badger Publishing

New words:

Rebels/rebel soldiers

soldiers fighting the government

Propeller

blades attached to a ship's engine to propel it through water

Mine-field

bombs hidden under the soil

Main characters:

Hero

Farad

CHAPTER 1
New Life

Mum looked at her new pups and wagged her tail. There were five of them. Three were brown and white and two were black. But wait! There was another – a tiny brown puppy the colour of sand.

Gently she pushed the tiny puppy closer to her milk.

"Drink up, little man," she said. "Then you'll grow big and strong and be a hero, just like your Dad."

And that's how Hero got his name.

But Hero didn't grow big and strong.
He stayed small and weak.

"Come on, Hero!" cried his brothers
and sisters. "Come and play with us!"

But Hero liked to sit near his Mum.
Together they watched the far
mountains change colour as the sun
rose over the dry earth.

"You must learn to be clever," said Hero's Mum. "Life is hard so you must be strong. But I will give you one piece of good advice – stay away from people. People are bad. They hate dogs. They are cruel and shout at us."

Hero listened.

CHAPTER 2

Fire in the Sky

Winter came and it was hard to find food. They were hungry.

Their Mum was gone for hours trying to find food. Hero's brothers and sisters got bored. They decided to try and find their own. Hero was left alone.

Suddenly a terrible noise filled Hero's ears. The sky was full of thunder and flames. He tried to run but the noise was everywhere. BOOM! BOOM!

He ran and ran. He ran until his paws hurt and he couldn't breathe. BOOM!

The noise got louder and fire lit up the sky. Smoke filled the air and the ground shook. BOOM! BOOM!

Hero saw a place to hide. He was shaking with fear.

Slowly the noise died away.

Hero wasn't alone. There was someone else. It was a human. A boy. But the boy didn't shout at Hero.

The boy didn't try to hurt Hero. Hero was amazed. The boy was scared... of him!

Hero wagged his tail slowly. The boy held out a trembling hand. Hero sniffed it then gave it a quick lick. It tasted salty because the boy had been crying.

The boy stroked Hero's head gently. Hero sat down next to the boy and snuggled up.

No words had been spoken, but they were friends.

CHAPTER 3
War

"My name is Farad," said the boy.
"I don't know where my family are.
When rebel soldiers came to our village
I was playing outside. The rebels
started shooting their guns in the air,
so I ran away. When I went back to the
village, everyone had gone. Now I'm
alone. Like you."

Hero didn't understand Farad's words
but he knew his voice was sad.

Just then they heard more human
voices. These ones were angry and
shouting. Hero was afraid.

Farad peeped through the doorway.

A man saw him.

"Hey! What are you doing in my house? Get out!"

"I'm sorry," said Farad. "I hid here when the planes dropped their bombs. I didn't know whose house it was."

"Well, you do now, so get out."

Hero growled. He didn't like people shouting at his new friend.

"Ugh! You brought a filthy dog into my house, too. How dare you?"

"He's my friend," said Farad bravely, even though he didn't feel very brave.

"Huh. Well, I think you'd better go," said the man. "Where is your family?"

"I don't know. I must try and find them," said Farad. "Perhaps they went to my cousin's village on the other side of the river. We'll try there first."

"Be careful. There are rebel soldiers everywhere."

The man turned his back. He had his own family to look after.

Farad walked away and Hero trotted next to him.

They had no food and no home – but they had each other.

The man watched them leave. "Watch out for mine-fields!" he shouted after them.

CHAPTER 4

Across the River

The river was wide and fast, but it wasn't very deep.

"I swam across this river in the Summer, but now it's Winter – it's freezing!"

Farad stared at the river.
"Let's walk down this side," said Farad.
"It might be less deep – I might be able to wade across."

They walked down river for a mile. Suddenly Hero growled low in his throat.

"What is it?" said Farad who had heard nothing. "Come on – this way."

But Hero wouldn't move. Instead he crouched down and bared his teeth.

"What's the matter?" said Farad, crossly.

Farad started to walk away but Hero grabbed his jacket and wouldn't let go.

"Stupid dog!" said Farad.

Hero was desperate. He tugged harder at Farad's jacket. Farad tripped and they both rolled down the river bank and into the cold mud at the bottom.

But Hero wasn't stupid. He knew exactly what he was doing – and he had just saved Farad's life.

"What was that noise?" said a man's voice.

"I didn't hear anything," said a second man. "It's probably just the river."

Three rebel soldiers with big guns were walking towards them. Another second and they would have seen Farad.

"No, I heard something," said the first man. "It could be more villagers – I'm going to look."

Farad pressed himself into the mud and hoped that the riverbank hid him. He could feel Hero next to him. Farad prayed hard.

The man peered down.

"Forget it!" called the second voice. "There's no-one there. They've all run away. They're all scared! Ha ha!"

The rebel soldiers sat down.

"There's a village on the other side of the river," said one. "Those people are against us."

"Anyone trying to hide there will have a nasty surprise!" said the second rebel.

"Yeah!" said the third. "A very loud, nasty surprise! Ha ha!"

They finished talking and strolled away.

Farad was shaking with fear.

"You saved me from those rebels!" he said.

Hero wagged his tail.

"We have to cross the river now in case they come back."

Farad waded into the river. It was icy cold. Hero dipped in a paw. He didn't like it and he backed away.

"Come on, you can do it!" shouted Farad.

Hero wasn't so sure.

"Come on, boy! Come on!"

Hero launched himself into the river and paddled hard. He tried to follow Farad but the current swept him away. He struggled to keep his head above water and his tail whirled like a propeller.

Farad made it across the river. He turned to look for his friend, but Hero had been swept away.

"Oh no!"

Farad ran down the riverbank and managed to get in front of Hero. He waded back into the river and caught him.

Poor Hero. He was coughing and spluttering. He had water in his eyes, in his ears and up his nose! He shook himself weakly and clambered into Farad's lap.

"I'm sorry!" said Farad. "I should have taken better care of you – you're so little!"

But Hero didn't care. He had saved his friend and now his friend had saved him.

"We can get to my cousin's village from here," said Farad. "We just have to cross these two fields and it's behind that hill."

Hero felt a bit wobbly after nearly drowning but he felt safe with Farad.

They walked through the first field but then Hero stopped and sniffed the wind.

"What is it?" said Farad. "Is it more rebel soldiers?"

But it was something even more dangerous.

Farad went to take a step forward but Hero grabbed his jacket in his teeth.

"Let go!" said Farad crossly. "We're nearly there!"

He took another step forward.

"Don't move!" yelled a voice.

Farad looked up.
"It's my cousin!"

"Don't take another step!" shouted his cousin. "You're in a mine-field!"

CHAPTER 5

Last Steps

Farad froze in his tracks.

"You're standing in a mine-field!" shouted his cousin. "If you take a wrong step you'll be blown up."

Farad was terrified.
"What shall I do?"

"Wait there," said his cousin. "I'll get help."

He ran back towards the village.

Soon more people came including Farad's uncle.

"Don't move, Farad!" cried his uncle.

"How are we going to get him out of there?" whispered Farad's cousin.
"If anyone tries to help him, they could be killed."

"I know, but we can't leave him there!" said Farad's uncle.

Hero didn't know what was going on but he knew that Farad had to get to his family.

He took one step forwards. Then another.

"What are you doing?" shouted Farad.

Hero couldn't explain. He looked up with his big, brown puppy eyes, begging Farad to trust him.

"You want me to follow you, don't you?" said Farad.

Slowly, carefully, Hero led Farad across the mine-field. He used his sensitive nose to sniff out where the mines were hidden.

Farad started to sweat even though the weather was cold.

"Look at that!" said Farad's cousin. "That dog is leading him across the mine-field! I think they're going to make it."

Step by step, paw by paw, Farad and Hero crossed the mine-field.

At last they reached the other side.

Farad threw himself into his uncle's arms.

"You're safe!" he said. "You're safe!"

"Yes," said Farad. "And this puppy saved me – he's a hero."

SNIFFER DOGS

- Dogs really can smell explosives. Some dog breeds have a sense of smell that is 2000 times more powerful than a person. This means they can smell and find things that are hidden.

- Police use sniffer dogs – also called 'detection dogs' – to find illegal drugs or explosives. One of the most popular breeds of dog for this work is the Springer Spaniel. Their name comes from the way they 'spring' or 'flush' out prey when working with huntsmen. They are friendly, happy dogs and also quick to learn. They have lots of stamina and can run and run.

30